THE FIERCE
YELLOW PUMPKIN

STORY BY MARGARET WISE BROWN

PICTURES BY RICHARD EGIELSKI

HARPERCOLLINSPUBLISHERS

THE FIERCE YELLOW PUMPKIN

Library of Congress Cataloging-in-Publication Data

Brown, Margaret Wise, 1910–1952.

The fierce yellow pumpkin / story by Margaret Wise Brown ; pictures by Richard Egielski.

p.   cm.

Summary: A little pumpkin dreams of the day when he will be a big, fierce,

yellow pumpkin who frightens away the field mice as the scarecrow does.

ISBN-10: 0-06-024479-8 (trade bdg.) – ISBN-13: 978-0-06-024479-8 (trade bdg.)

ISBN-10: 0-06-024481-X (lib. bdg.) – ISBN-13: 978-0-06-024481-1 (lib. bdg.)

ISBN-10: 0-06-443534-2 (pbk.) – ISBN-13: 978-0-06-443534-5 (pbk.)

[1. Pumpkin–Fiction.   2. Jack-o-lanterns–Fiction.   3. Halloween–Fiction.]

I. Egielski, Richard, ill.   II. Title.

PZ7.B8163 Ff   2003   2002008338   [E]–dc21

Typography by Al Cetta

❖

First Edition

There was once a small pumpkin in a great big field, a very small green pumpkin the size of an apple. The fierce sun burned down on the little pumpkin, and he grew and grew. And pretty soon there was a fat little, round little, yellow little pumpkin in a great big field.

Now, this fat little, round little, yellow little pumpkin grew so fat and full of himself that he began to think he was a very fierce vegetable, as fierce as the sun that warmed his fat round sides. "Ho! Ho! Ho!" he would say. "When I grow up, I will scare the field mice out of the field like the scarecrow does."

The little pumpkin would dearly have loved to make a fierce, ferocious gobble-gobble face like the scarecrow's at the far end of the field. But try as he would, his own pumpkin face stayed smooth and yellow and shining.

Then one day the sun did not shine as hot as fire. And blackbirds, skies full of blackbirds, began flying over the big field. There was a burning smell of leaves in the air and a crisp tingle that tickled the fat little pumpkin's sides. There were so many birds in the sky that the scarecrow was busy from before daylight until after daylight, chasing the birds out of his field.

His gobble-gobble face became droopy and dreadful. The wind blew *whoo* through his hair. He lost one scarecrow eye. The old scarecrow knew that if there is anything that a blackbird is scared of, it is a one-eyed scarecrow!

But then that night and the night after, something began to happen. The first cold frosts came in the night. And the fat little, round little, yellow little pumpkin woke up one morning and discovered that he was a fiery orange-yellow pumpkin. The color of the sun. A fierce, burning color.

Then three little children came galloping through the big field past the old one-eyed scarecrow. They ran right up to the fat little, round little, orange little pumpkin, and one little girl called out, "Here he is. Here is our terrible pumpkin!"

So they cut the pumpkin's heavy stem with a little saw knife. Each taking turns, they carried the pumpkin home, across the field to their house. The little pumpkin liked that.

And then with the little saw knife they hollowed him out all empty inside, sweet smelling and clean as a whistle. Then they cut one big round eye in the side of his face. A big round hole. And the little pumpkin liked that.

"Ho! Ho!" laughed the pumpkin.

The fierce yellow pumpkin.

"I'm a one-eyed pumpkin for sure."

Then they cut another big round hole in the other side of his face.

"Ho! Ho!" laughed the pumpkin.

The fierce yellow pumpkin.

"I'm a fierce yellow pumpkin

for sure."

But that wasn't all. The children cut a sharp shape in the pumpkin for a nose, the shape of a witch's hat. And that wasn't all, either. They took the little saw knife and they sawed zigzag up and zigzag down until the pumpkin had a whole mouth full of sharp zigzag teeth.

Then with a loud *Ho! Ho!* the little pumpkin laughed a dreadful zigzag laugh across his zigzag teeth.

"Ho, ho, ho!

He, he, he!

Mice will run

when they see me."

He was certainly a fierce and ferocious pumpkin with a terrific, terrible face.

After a while it was night. There was black darkness all around, inky black darkness.

The children came in with a lighted candle and stuck it inside the pumpkin so that the light shined out his big round eyes and his triangle nose. And the light shined over his zigzag teeth. He was a horrible sight to see. *Grrrrr* in the dark. He grinned a zigzag grin there in the corner of the porch. *Grrrrr.*

And the children danced about him, singing a song to the terrific, terrible pumpkin with the zigzag grin.

And the little pumpkin was fierce and happy, and
he sang:
   "Ho, ho, ho!
   He, he, he!
   Mice will run
   when they see me!"

And they did.